To:_____

From:_____

Big Bird's Big Bad Day

a story about
turning frowns
upside down

words by Craig Manning • pictures by Joe Mathieu

Some days are perfect, and some are okay,
but for Big Bird, today was a *very* bad day.
It started off cloudy and dreary and gray,
and nobody wanted to come out and play.

Soon heavy raindrops started to fall.

It wasn't nice weather to go and play ball.

Big Bird made breakfast, not feeling his best,
and then he spilled milk all over his nest.

He cleaned up the spill until it was dry,
then sat down and grumbled and let out a sigh.
He thought that at least things would get better soon
when Granny Bird visited that afternoon!

But Granny Bird canceled because she felt ill.
She had a bad cough and complained of a chill.

Then poor Big Bird lost his favorite stuffed bear!
He couldn't find it—he had looked everywhere!

Big Bird was upset and he didn't quite know
the right word for why he was feeling so low.
And what could he do with these feelings he had?
How could he make himself not feel so sad?

SAD

GLOOMY

disappointed

CONFUSED

Blue

Then Elmo arrived and asked what was wrong,
since Big Bird looked like he'd heard a sad song.
"I'm having a bad day," Big Bird said with a cry.
"I'm feeling so gloomy, and I don't know why."

"You need a hug," Elmo said right away.
He knew how it felt to have such a hard day.
"What Mommy tells Elmo is always to share
the way you are feeling with people who care."

And so off they went for a walk around town
to find out how others turned frowns upside down.
When the Count is upset, which happens now and then,
he takes a short break and counts up to ten.

1 2 3 4 5 6 7 8 9 10

How about Cookie Monster? What does he do
when he's feeling sad, or lonely, or blue?

"Me thinks a distraction can help you feel better.
Try baking some cookies, or knitting a sweater!"

When Big Bird told Rosita how he was feeling,
she knew just the way to help with his healing.
"A song about joy, celebration, and fun
can send away clouds and bring back the sun!"

But what if a song alone won't do the trick?

What if those sad feelings just want to stick?

Big Bird asked Zoe if she knew, by chance,

and she said, "Just pair a good song with a dance!"

So, when you're feeling blue and down in the dumps
there's a surefire way to stop being a grump.
"I get active," said Oscar. "I roll in the trash.
If you skip, run, or play, you'll cheer up in a flash!"

Big Bird felt better, but the day wasn't over,
and Elmo still thought they should go talk to Grover.

How did he handle sadness
when it came along?

He said, "Helping others makes *me* happy and strong!"

And now, at last Big Bird was starting to see
just how good his bad day could turn out to be!
He even played ball with his friends Bert and Ernie,
a beautiful end to his long, winding journey.

Some days *aren't* perfect, so Big Bird had found.
Today had been bad, but his mood turned around!

With friends there to sing and to dance and play ball,
Big Bird's big bad day wasn't so bad after all!

Published by Sourcebooks Wonderland, an imprint of Sourcebooks Kids
P.O. Box 4410, Naperville, Illinois 60567–4410
(630) 961-3900
sourcebookskids.com

Source of Production: Shenzhen Wing King Tong Paper Products Co. Ltd.,
Shenzhen, Guangdong Province, China
Date of Production: December 2019
Run Number: 5017526

Printed and bound in China.
WKT 10 9 8 7 6 5 4 3 2